Half-Crown Bob

HALF-CROWN BOB

A sketch, a story and a letter

Price Warung

BONFIRE BOOKS

Published 2021 by Bonfire Books

First published by George Robertson & Co. in *Half-Crown Bob and Tales of the Riverine* (1898) by Price Warung (William Astley)

Introduction and editorial matter © Lucas Smith 2021

ISBN: 978-0-6450664-0-1

Bonfire Books
bonfirebooks.org

Cover image: "I Have Got It" (1854)-Eugene von Guerard

Also by Price Warung from Bonfire Books:

Selected Tales of Price Warung (2020)

Contents

To "Lois"
A simple acknowledgement of a devoted life

INTRODUCTION

By Lucas Smith

HALF-CROWN BOB IS THE LONGEST WORK of fiction by
William Astley, who wrote under the pseudonym,
chosen for its Aboriginal undertones, of Price Warung.
Astley completed nearly all of his work in the 1890s, a
time in Australia when the scattered colonies were
discovering and creating a cultural identity distinct from
Great Britain. Australian literature flourished as Henry
Lawson, Barbara Baynton, Banjo Paterson and many
others found a distinctly Antipodean style. Warung was
published alongside them, primarily in the Sydney
Bulletin, the weekly newspaper which was the main
clearinghouse for Australian writers in those boom times.

The majority of Warung's stories are about the convict era of Australian history and many of them are very dark indeed, exaggerating the charnel-house particulars and systemic cruelty of those times (see *Selected Tales of Price Warung* (2020), published by Bonfire Books). In *Half-Crown Bob*, Warung, usually so unsentimental in his depictions of the mutually reinforcing cruelties of transport and overseer, turns his hand to a domestic drama. Robert Strathing, a wealthy young Englishman, taking a tour of the continent before he is to begin a steady career in the family firm, is called suddenly back to London from recreation in Monte Carlo. The events that give Robert his mysterious moniker 'Half-Crown' and end with his death on the Victorian goldfields, form the bulk of the story. The novella was serialised in the *Bulletin* and published in 1898 alongside several stories about early steamboat traffic on the Murray River as *Half-Crown Bob and Tales of the Riverine*.

Structurally, the novel begins indirectly with 'The Sketch': Bob *in media res* on the goldfields, hinting at the mysteries to be resolved in 'The Story': the domestic drama that precedes 'The Sketch'. The tale ends with 'The Letter': written after Bob's death to Bob's father by the goldfields pharmacist Pestle, the only man who knew Bob's real name.

The kind of personal honour that Warung portrays and that obtained not even 150 years ago, at least as an ideal, may seem implausible to contemporary readers, used to a world of broken promises where predatory lenders are bailed out by governments and politicians use their offices as bordellos and bathhouses. Probably most of us have never known such loyalty as Strathing *fils* shows to Strathing *pere*. The womanly fidelity of Lois also contains a touch of absurdity. Why should she, wholly blameless in the drama, sacrifice everything, even if it is of her own free choice? Surely the calculation of greatest good for greatest number suggests that she is naïve at best and deranged at worst. Bob's death scene brings to mind Oscar Wilde's famous quip that one must have a heart of stone not to laugh at the death of Little Nell. And yet there is no hint of insincerity or ironic distance in Warung's prose. In their irrevocable choices of voluntary disgrace, emigration and chastity, the characters in this world, not very distant in time from our own, obtain true meaning. Nineteenth century Australia is still a recognisable world in many ways but as regards honour and fidelity, a cynical response to Bob and Lois' sacrifice says much about us, little of it good.

Half-Crown Bob is also notable as a minor repository of obsolete Australian slang, which has always been ephemeral and embedded in local context. The particular circumstances of 19th century goldrush life led to a proliferation of new words. Several of these have been noted by me, indicated in the footnotes with '(ed.)'.

Price Warung wrote primarily for a print-mad colonial society. He wrote quickly and for money. So did Dickens and so did Warung's greater—it must be said—contemporary, Lawson. Here, as in many other cases, the constraints of haste, led to something lasting, where many of the more polished works of the time by people of leisure feel stale or stillborn. Look at 'old Half-Crown' and see an ideal man and contemplate whether he is so unbelievable as he may seem.

Melbourne, April 2021

Lucas Smith is a writer and graduate student and co-founder of Bonfire Books.

Half-Crown Bob

THE SKETCH

NOBODY KNEW WHO first gave him the sobriquet. He did not know himself, and, as he once said, "it fitted him, so he didn't care." Nor was anybody any better informed as to the exact time that Robert Strathing lost his identity in "Half-Crown Bob." Many were the discussions when more exciting topics were scarce, as to whether Bob's nickname arrived with him when he made his appearance on Pleasant Creek, or whether it was of purely local origin, and owed nothing of its appropriateness to Ararat or the other goldfields previously honoured by Bob's presence.

Once indeed, when a tremendous fall of rain prevented work at the claims for some days, and every other controverted point in the camp politics, sociology and theology, had been thrashed out at Pat Davey's shanty, the bar of which served not only for spirituous refreshment for the inner man, but also as the arena for contests of all sorts—from the kind regulated by the code of the P.R.[1] to that controlled by vague reminiscences of Parliamentary procedure—a row royal took place on this latter question. A new-comer from a Southern diggings, prompted by recklessness and the juice of the great Western grape, had asserted that the whole of the Pleasant Creek populace didn't contain enough mental capacity to devise so characteristic a name. Ararat, he thought, might be clever enough to do it, but he doubted even Ararat. In his judgment, so happy an epithet could only be the offspring of Ballarat genius—Ballarat, the big

---

[1] Unclear reference, probably refers to "Penal Reform", meaning the "Bloody Code" which mandated the death penalty for around 200 criminal offenses (ed.)

and brilliant. Of course, this slur on the inventiveness of the Creek people could not be allowed to pass unresented. The new-comer was hotly supported by other late arrivals, from what was, even in these early months of the "sixties," generally styled "The Golden City." To them were joined men who had matriculated in their mining career at Ararat, at Forest Creek, and on the Waranga, and who, caring little for Ballarat, cared less for the Creek field.

Quite a formidable band of combatants were all these, but the indignant defenders of the Creek reputation were as numerically and physically strong. The result was a contest which was epochal even in a period when no day passed without its battle; but as the parties were equally matched, victory could not be truthfully said to rest with either side. And it was perhaps better so, for, leaving the original problem unsolved, it also left a decent excuse for another fight on a future occasion. There were, to be sure, some hasty brains and impetuous souls who wanted the matter settled one way or the other. These were, however, so few as to be powerless. With them must be classed Bob himself, though he was neither hasty-brained nor impetuous-souled. Bob, it has been hinted, didn't object to the qualifying term, without which he was never spoken of, and seldom addressed, but he did object in his heart to being bothered about its origin and the place of its birth.

And though he was one of the most peaceable creatures living, he rejoiced at the fight because he believed it would have the effect of determining, once for all, where he had won his title. Some men would have been proud to have been the primary cause of such a combat, and prouder still to think that other collisions were imminent for precisely the same reason. Bob was, however, different. He never gave a thought to the personal honour done to himself. His interest in the fight and his regret that it had not "gone to a finish"—apart from its making a break in a rather dreary and monotonous week—were untinged by selfish gratification. It took up his time to have to reply to people who asked him how and when and where he came by his name, that knew almost as much about it before they asked as he did, and his time, he used to say, was really not his own. That was the basis of his hope that the fight would settle the whole thing, for, of course, the victory of either side would have been tantamount to a decision as to the locality at least whence he had gained his sobriquet.

It seems, looking back on these olden and golden days, a trivial thing to have excited so much curiosity, stirred up so many fights, prompted such lots of apparently impertinent questioning. Only a nickname! But the men who lived the life of those ancient digging days—and life was worth living then—knew that nothing was trivial. The frivolity of their behaviour and the commonplace of their talk were simply the safety-valves of an intense existence. Men who would else have gone mad or to the devil, had their sanity or moral equilibrium preserved by trifles. A great colonial Judge once remarked that he was only saved from becoming a mental wreck, at the height of his gold-madness, by carving cherry-stones which he had ridden nearly two hundred miles to obtain. Trifles that were nothing but trifles— trifles behind which stood great facts and solemn truths— these made up the leisure life of the miners on the early goldfields. Now, "Half-Crown Bob," the nick-name, was a trifle; but it was a trifle behind which there was an important and interesting fact—"Half-Crown Bob," the man.

Once people knew the man, they ceased to wonder at the fictitious name suggesting inquiry and curiosity. There was a young Petre, for instance—a scion of the noble English house—who forgot all the traditional reverence for the saints canonized by the Mother of all Churches, and put the martyrs and confessors to no better use than to swear by—how he sneered when, on his first evening in camp, his tent-mates spent most of the hours in debating about Bob's name, and Bob himself! (His mates, by the way, were Clarendon, formerly of the 10th Hussars, and who had made one of the gallant troop who had ridden up Balaclava valley, and Tilbury, the son of a bishop, whose enormous influence did not suffice to save his boy from merited University disgrace.) But after he, Petre, met him, Bob, the next day, how resolutely he entered upon the quest of discovering all about Bob and all about his name. Not in an impertinent fashion, mind you. Petre, though a ne'er-do-well, and the seventy-fold returned prodigal, who would yet make his seventy-first journey in search of the husks, was still a gentleman, and would not have poked the tip of his bejewelled little finger into another man's affairs against his will. But Petre had been impressed by Bob, as everybody was impressed who came in contact with him. And by that "everybody" you must please understand everybody—from the old Van Demonian "lag" who was cook at Ledcourt, the neighbouring cattle station, to the aristocratic gold-commissioner who dwelt on or did occasional business with the Creek.

All knew Bob. The newest chum, who came but yesterday, the lightest-winged (and luggaged) bird of passage, who, being usually of the hawk variety, found it desirable to stay no longer than a day or so on the Creek; the "oldest inhabitant," who came with the first rush, and who had determined to stay until he had "panned-out,"— all knew him, and loved him. It's a strange thing to say of the fluctuating fifteen thousand people or so who made up the Pleasant Creek population in the early "sixties," that they all knew and loved a young fellow who had no other name than "Half-Crown Bob," and whose antecedents were enwrapped in mystery. It's a strange thing, but a true one.

"To know such and such an one is to love him," is a phrase heard not seldom; and when it is used, one of two things may generally be predicted: either that the "him" is a "her," or that the loveworthy personality is known to but a few, and them only of his own class. Said of "Half-Crown Bob," the words meant much more. From first to last Bob must have made the acquaintance of twenty thousand adults and children more or less "grown-up" during his sojourn on the Creek. Perhaps it would be more accurate to say that that number had made Bob's acquaintance. It was part of the ceremony attached to the reception of every fresh arrival that he, she, or it should be taken and shown Bob's claim and tent, and their owner if visible. It mattered not whether the new-comer was an old hand at digging, or whether the he, she, or it (why don't the grammarians invent a compound gender?) had been so short a time in the Colony that the sea air still lingered in his, her, or its clothing, and the ship's motion was still visible in his, her, or its gait. All had to go, willy-nilly, and be shown "Half-Crown Bob's" habitat.

"Been to see Half-Crown Bob's place yet?" queried a couple of "the boys" one day of a surly-looking fellow as he was driving in the last peg for his just-erected tent.

"—yer, no, I haven't, and don't want ter,—yer!" was the sulky but emphatic response of the tent-pegger, as, rising, he turned defiantly on his interrogators.

"Don't want ter, don't yer? Well, we'll see about that. Yer see, my dear friend," and the speaker's eyes twinkled dangerously, as he used, it is to be suspected ironically, the insinuating phrase, "it just 'appens to be a sort of rule of these diggin's that everybody 'as got to be interdooced to that gent as I've just named. So come 'long!'"

The tent-pegger was an old Pacific Slope man[2] of the picturesque "Forty" period. Many a muss had he been into and got out of with credit to himself and damage to his adversary, and the "beads" he had drawn and the men he had "dropped" formed not the least despicable amongst the records of the duello[3] as practised by the Argonauts. As he rose to his full length, a very ugly customer he looked. During the exhortation to come and be "interdooced" he had shortened his grasp on the billet of firewood which served him for a mallet; and, as the exhorter ended in what were doubtless intended to be persuasive accents, but which, unfortunately, suggested formidable consequences in case the invitation was declined, the billet flew straight for the exhorter's head. It was followed by a condensed Commination service. Despoiled of its objurgatory ornaments, the language of the service implied that the billet-thrower hadn't the slightest idea of "coming 'long"; and, what was more, he

[2] A Californian (ed.)
[3] The practice of duelling (ed.)

would make it particularly hot for anybody who persisted in asking him.

What was the sequel will take longer to tell than it did to happen. It was Bill the Smelter who, wishing to be neighbourly, had proposed to "interdooce" the latest arrival. It was Bill the Smelter who had made the exhortation above reported. It was the same Bill the Smelter who, owing to old-time expertness at "mid-on" in the cricket-fields in his native Kent, had caught the piece of wood as it hurtled fearfully close to his head, and let the sender "have it" before the lapse of a second full on the left leg, a couple of inches below the knee.

"I think yer'll come 'long now an' be interdooced," said Bill, as the ex-Argonaut fell (the limb was broken), easing his descent by more extracts from the damnatory clauses. And the ex-Argonaut was introduced straight away, being carried to Half-Crown's claim in his own blanket, from a fold of which Bill took the precaution to remove something known in camp parlance as "shooting-irons."

When Bob heard the story he turned his back on Bill and refused to speak to him. He set the fractured limb—he had picked up a knowledge of bone-setting in his college days—and with his gentle touch and kindly smile soon broke through the crust that overlaid the Californian's heart, and made him thankful after all that he had been "interdooced"—so thankful, indeed, that he abandoned his resolve to shoot Bill on sight.

As for Bill, the fact that he suffered keenly from being under Bob's displeasure did not make him the less ardent in "interdoocin'" people. It must be said, though (so that Bill shall not obtain too much credit), that there never was any occasion to resort to extreme measures with any subsequent comers. Anybody who was unconsciously about to follow the example of the Californian, and had an objection to be "interdooced," was forthwith told of the billet-cum-broken-leg episode, and the narrative had the invariable effect of cancelling all objections. In fact, everybody was the better for knowing or only seeing Bob, and, what was more, every one knew and felt as much: and everybody included representatives of every type of human nature and every nationality under the sun. Not Bob's own class only, unless, as Petre once remarked to a Tilburnian[4] ejaculation, "Wonder what was Bob's 'set' at home?" "Bob's set then! God knows! And He knows now that Bob's set includes every soul upon the field. I don't know whether it's wrong, lads" (Clarendon was present besides Tilbury), "and I don't care, but I often think when Christ comes again He'll hold Right D. 27,964." From which it may be seen that much eating of husks had not totally destroyed Petre's perception of good, though certainly the reference to Bob's miner's right smacked of irreverence.

---

[4] Alternative spelling of 'Tyburnian', referring to the village of Tyburn, traditional site of criminal hangings in London (ed.)

A unique personality it must have been to have thus attracted all sorts and conditions of men. Let us see what its outer shell was like. A strongly-built but lithe form, bold, with an erectness that seemed to add to its more than average height, was crowned with a massive head, round which clustered crispy curls of dark hair and beard. The head looked, in profile, that of a handsome man, its contour was so clear-cut. But gazing straight into Bob's face you would never consider him handsome. There was a broad, high forehead, but it was seared with lines of thought and anxiety that had no right to be there if mere years went for anything. There was a long, delicately-curved nose, with nostrils that dilated in passion. There were a mouth and a chin that meant strength, and yet were features wherein it seemed laughter and smiles would, had affairs gone well, loved to have nestled. All the elements of manly beauty, one thought, and yet the face was not a handsome one. Why? The eyes answered the question.

Sunk to an unnatural depth, they spoilt the aspect of the whole face, or you thought they did, until you discovered that they were not so deeply sunk but that you could fathom in their depths a quality of their own. And once you saw that—and nobody who took a second look at Bob could help seeing or feeling it—you forgot all about the other features, and how they lost their effect through the singularity of the eyes. You saw only the eyes and the soul, the greatly-tortured but magnanimous and tolerant soul that used them for its windows, and looked through them on to the world that had used their owner so cruelly. Of course, every man Jack or woman Jill of those who gazed into Bob's eyes could not perceive all this, but those who did not, felt it, as has been said. Anyhow, all understood it. As if by instinct, all knew that Bob had passed through an awfulness of trouble that would have killed most men, and was even then carrying a burden that perhaps not one of the many strong and true men on the Creek could have borne and remained sane.

It was one of the most inexplicable things how this idea spread and got a universal grip on the Creek populace. Intellectual clods absorbed it in their dull brains; preternaturally sharp fellows, who were born with razor-edged wits, and who had kept up their fineness by incessant attrition with the legal forces of civilization, mastered it no sooner. This was the secret of Bob's influence, and the reason everybody loved him; everybody knew that he had suffered beyond the suffering of all others there; and they knew, too, that not an atom of a noble nature had been warped or destroyed in the refining fire. The simple felt that if trouble overtook them—and trouble and sickness and death always held big liens on the early goldfields—Bob was there with his advice and help. The weak, while struggling with their weakness, and recognizing that they must yield, had a blind faith in Bob's power to rescue them from the consequence of their folly. The knavish also believed that Bob, if consulted in the terror of the moment, when the approach of Nemesis was expected, would never "put them away." He might advise restitution where restitution was possible; he hated sin, and he hated crime, sometimes more, sometimes less, than sin to which legal penalty attached, and he had no sympathy for the sinner when he was not a repented sinner. But his knowledge with the world, his potency with the mass, and with the constituted authorities of the district, were all at the service of any poor wretch who, law-hunted or remorse-driven, hungered for a city-refuge. The humble felt that Bob was an impregnable shield against the tyranny of self-created or state-created powers, while the latter, if not the former, well knew they had in him an efficacious ally in the preservation of order and the regulation of the township and its vicinage.

At the critical moment when Law ranged itself on the side of Injustice, and did its best to facilitate the success of the gang which jumped Ditchburn and party's claim in the very richest part of the lead, it was Bob who saved the resort to shooting-irons, and another Eureka affair, and brought the round dozen of troopers from the midst of the infuriated mob. It was Bob who suspected that the informalities in Ditchburn's papers were somehow connected with the circumstance that the leader of the jumpers was brother-in-law to the Commissioner's clerk, and who suggested to the said clerk that an immediate resignation might prevent the sudden dislocation of his neck. Who was it that freed young Spiffles, the brainless fool, fresh from a Liverpool counting-house, who, in an inebriated hour, had been married, not so much to as by one Liz, a lady upon whose reputation a dab of tar would have appeared, by contrast, nearly white, but Bob? Bob it was, again, who made Smithson, a cadet of a banking family, whose honours included hereditary legislative as well as financial trophies, marry the girl who had followed him from London in the desperation of her not wise love. And was it not the same all-round healer of wounds and redresser of grievances who, when Jock Lung's, the splitter's, five-year-old tot strayed from the hut at the base of the Grampians, organized and led the search parties, and was himself so long away that the parties were forming to search for him, when he re-appeared with the dead child in his arms? Was it not he, too, that washed the dead child and prepared it for its tiny grave, its mother the while lying in a death-like faint, and its father putting, with gentle "tap-tap," the roofing shingles together for the "little un's" coffin? And of course it was Bob, and no one else, the chap who came up when the February of '61[5] escort was stuck up near the Western, just as the troopers were getting the worst of it, and helped them to turn the tables and arrest the ringleaders. Apparently, too, the trifling circumstance that the same chap (in other words Bob) carried away on his shoulder from the scene of the attack one of the raiding party's bullets did not prevent him from exerting himself to obtain the ablest Melbourne constable—Aspinall, it was—in order that the raider's life might be spared from the gallows, not for the raider's sake exactly, but for that of the grey-haired old lady in Sydney, whose son of many prayers would have gone to a quicklime grave in Ballarat but for Bob.

"Half-Crown Bob," said old Pestle the Quaker chemist and official pluralist, "the worst I can say of him is that people rush into trouble on purpose that Bob can comfort 'em and help 'em out!" And old Pestle, not that he was old, by any means—he was only big-brained and long-headed-was right. It was difficult—almost impossible—to get very intimate with Bob, unless one was in trouble. As a rule, the bigger the trouble the greater the intimacy.

There was one exception to this rule, however. That was in the case of delicately nurtured Locke, who fell home-sick, and hungered after his mother's and his

---

[5] Soldiers who put down the Lambing Flats riots (ed.)

sister's caressing. He was boy enough to wish he could go home by the first vessel, but he was man enough to stick to his claim, in the hope that, when he did go, he would own the wherewithal to make life easier and brighter for the dear ones who were praying and dreaming of him by day and night.

Well, Locke was going mad, really mad, for want of some one to open his heart to. He went to Bob.

"What's the trouble, lad? Something wrong, I see," spoke out old Half-Crown at once.

When it came to the pinch, Locke could not confess there was nothing more wrong with him than home-sickness, so replied—

"Oh, nothing, Half-Crown; was passing and thought I'd see how you were. That's all!" and so he took himself off with his heart full. It was Bob's shift at the windlass, and his mate had that moment signalled to haul, so he could not follow the lad to see what was really up, but he felt sure that he would know before long. And he did. Locke went his miserable way to his tent when a bright thought struck him. He would go and gamble with Palmetto Jack, the New Orleans cardsharper. He could not lose much; the English mail had gone the previous week, and had taken away all his net earnings to date; but still he had enough to lose to justify his returning to Bob and making a lament over his weakness, and his disregard of his mother's wish that he should never gamble.

Palmetto Jack was soon found, and soon the ten-pennyweight nugget, and ounce of "dust," which represented Locke's work for the week, were transferred to that worthy per the agency of poker. It was very wrong and very weak of the lad, no doubt, and so Bob told him, when he confessed to gambling the same night; but what a glorious talk it caused, how skilfully the older man led the younger one on till the latter's heart was bared, and the innermost spring of his home-sickness at last welled forth in Bob's clear vision. And how intently did the lad (he was only twenty-one) listen, as dear Half-Crown urged him, as he valued his future here and his future in the hereafter, to be true to his mother and his sisters.

"God alone knows," said Bob, "all that our women suffer on our account, the ceaseless agony of prayer, the dreadful humiliation and horror when we do wrong, the nameless fears that even when we do right we do it by accident and not by principle. The heaped-up sin of all the women who ever lived can be as nothing beside the pangs men have made women suffer in their pride and their recklessness and their evil-doing. Thank God, Locke, that you have such a woman to pray for you—three such women. If you don't win heaven with that help, you must be an infernal scamp. I have two—"

But here Half-Crown broke down, as no one on the Creek ever saw him before or after. Locke "cleared" then, and before he turned into his blankets that night he did what he had left undone for many a day. He said his prayers; and thanked God for his mothers and his sisters, and Bob. He did not pray to get his money back from the professor of poker; but he got it back for all that, for Palmetto Jack had an interview with Bob the next day, which left an impression on his mind that it would be the cheapest in the long run to refund his winnings. He never had a chance to regain them, for Locke was afterwards watched by Bob closely, and Locke sometimes smiled to himself at thinking how cheaply he won Bob's intimacy. But the lad forgot that his trouble had been very big and very real at the time. Old Pestle, to whom in after years he told the story, understood perfectly well that the boy must have been in distress, and took the incident as additional evidence (though none was needed) in support of his own belief that people purposely plunged into trouble that they might be pulled out by Bob.

Old Pestle was never in trouble himself, but he emulated Bob in bearing as many of his neighbours' as he could, and thus had a sort of vicarious claim on Half-Crown's sympathy. He had a claim of his own upon Bob's intimacy, but this was quite unconnected with trouble (unless it was Bob's private sorrows), but he never cared to advance it.

How it arose was in this way. When Bob first came to the Creek, he was a store-hand and had no need to "register." He waited to look about a bit before he marked out his claim. When he put in his pegs old Pestle was acting as mining registrar—he was always "acting" something or other, was Pestle. "Old right?" queried the acting-registrar. "Date out, and mislaid!" as laconically replied Bob. "Name?" once more queried the representative of the Government. Bob hesitated. Pestle looked up, and saw in Bob's face the reflection of a struggle between the disgrace of an alias and a desire to conceal his identity. "Call you Smith; no, too many Smiths already; Jones, Brown, Robinson, all the same fault. Haven't you a nickname?" For a Quaker Pestle had a very flexible tongue and keen apprehension. "Well," stammered Bob, "I have sometimes been called 'Half-Crown Bob!'" "That'll do—H. C. Bob!" And that's how old Pestle had a claim on Bob's intimacy and "all the privileges and rights appertaining thereto." Moreover, that's how it came about that when miners of an inquisitive sort thought they would satisfy themselves of Bob's real name by a glance at the register of his claim and "right," they received nothing for the shilling they had to disburse for permission to inspect the record but "H. C. Bob."

It used to be a favourite dodge played on new hands, when they were anxious, as they almost invariably were, about Bob's identity, for the oldsters to send them up to Pestle to look through the registers. The fellow who invented it subsequently courted Pestle's daughter and married her, the freed cynics alleging that the only reason Pestle consented to the match being the number of shilling inspection fees he obtained through his prospective son-in-law's ready-wittedness.

The mystery surrounding Half-Crown was also a constant source of income to Pat Davey and other bar-keepers and shanty-owners. No new arrival thought he had done his duty to Bob and to himself till he had first shouted for the whole staff of the post-office, and plied them with questions and drink as to whether Bob ever got letters and papers, and if so, how they were addressed; or till he had fortified himself with liquor sufficient to float his courage to the point of saying to Bob something like this:—

"I say, Half-Crown, tell us how you got that queer name of yours; there must be a big yarn hanging to it— ain't there? And while you're about it, can't you tell us something about yourself, old man? You know, we think so much of you, we'd like to know all about you."

All this, of course, was very rude and very annoying, and if we were telling a fiction instead of a true story, we would make Bob rise up in wrath and retaliate on impertinent interrogator No. 1 with a revolver so effectually that there would be no impertinent interrogator No. 2.

Truth to tell, Bob did raise, not his revolver, but his eyebrows, the first time this kind of question was put to him, and felt somewhat vexed. It had become a habit with him in his self-communings to think quickly, and so he thought quickly now, and spoke slowly, where most men would have reversed the processes. And when he spoke he uttered the words: "You want to know all about me and my name, do you? Well, I don't think it would do you any good to tell you, and I'm certain it would make me feel bad, so you'll have to excuse me. But I don't mind telling you about my nick-name; that is, all I know—I can't tell you more, can I?" looking pleasantly up at the silent circle surrounding his hole. Then, after a pause, he resumed:—

"How I came to be called 'Half-Crown Bob' I don't know; who stood god-father I don't know; nor where it first stuck to me. But it fits me, and I'll tell you—it may do some of you fellows good—that I promised a dear lady in the old land, that till I succeeded in doing a certain thing, I would live upon half-a-crown a week, or as near thereto as possible. Now, boys, you know that few in this new country can make it possible to live upon half-a-crown a day, to say nothing of a week. But I've kept my promise in the spirit if not to the letter. I've mentioned this thing once or twice before I came to the Creek, and I suppose my nickname came about through my doing so. That's all I can tell you!" And before any one could say anything, he had sprung out of his hole—very shallow it was then—and strode away to his tent.

The listeners turned from his claim, none breaking the silence, till a lanky cornstalk remarked that "that 'ere darned Grampian mist must be hanging about the camp, as it had got into his eyes;" an oracular utterance to which his comrades sniffed assent. By sniffing, instead of speaking, they perhaps thought to avert the penalty of lying, for the cornstalk most certainly didn't speak the truth about the mist. The summits of the Grampians, fourteen miles away, wore a sun-woven coronet that glittered and glanced in the pellucid blue of a summer sky. What mist there was in his eyes was due to Bob's few words, and the sinners knew it.

Bob's reply became historic. Every one in camp and township, up at the reefs at the east, down Commercial Street at the west, and along the full length of straggling Main Street, which was the connecting link between the Occident and the Orient, heard of it before ten o'clock that night, and always remembered it afterwards. People the next time they saw Bob, noticed in him something more worthy of respect. At least, they fancied so; the truth was, they had learnt something from his words which had made them more capable of seeing the pure strength of his nature. And now was displayed a very curious thing. This heterogeneous mass became homogeneous where Bob was concerned.

Each of the thousands who heard of his reply that night seemed the next day to have come to regard it as a confidence made to himself or herself personally, and to only one or two mutual friends besides. They would talk about Bob to the new-comers that flocked to the field, sometimes at the rate of a score a day, sometimes by hundreds—once, when Chamber's flat lead was bottomed upon, the increase tallied into thousands. They would mysteriously hint at the mystery surrounding the man and his name; but the whetted curiosity of the immigrant, however ingeniously worded, would obtain no further insight into Half-Crown's affairs than the assurance that, if inquiry were made of Bob himself, he would tell a stranger just as much as the oldsters knew— which, of course, was no more and no less than the truth. Old Pestle, who, Quakerism notwithstanding, was a social philosopher of the Herbert Spencer school, used in after years to include the promptitude with which the units of the current Creek population came to the conclusion that Bob's reply was for their ears only, as the most extraordinary of the many peculiar phenomena of goldfield life.

As for Bob himself, the question came so often afterwards, that he stereotyped, so to speak, his answer. He made one alteration, however, in its phrasing. For the "dear lady," a phrase too tender to pass his lips often, he substituted "a dear friend." But there was that in his tone which indicated the sex of the friend all the same. It was painfully wearisome to him, this questioning, but in time he saw that, through it, his influence spread, and he was wishful that his influence—which, not being a fool, he was aware made for truth and order—showed wider day by day. He thought, perhaps, that the wrong for which he suffered might be the sooner atoned for.

Why his influence should spread was, however, a problem which, being modest withal, he could not solve. It was a constant marvel to him, this dear old Half-Crown, that people should flock to him, do as he told them, love him. Being, as we said, not a fool, he knew they did these things; but why—that he did not know. We know; it was because of the soul in his eyes.

THE STORY

"COME HOME, ROBERT, my son, at once. I want you badly. Life or death, come direct to the bank."

These were the words that met Bob Strathing's eyes as he tore open a telegram posted on from his latest Paris

address to the Hôtel de Paris, Monte Carlo. Bob was
standing in the Casino grounds at a spot overlooking the
Mediterranean expanse when he read them. He had been
handed his letters as he left the hotel for his morning
stroll, but he delayed opening them till he could find a
restful nook near the sea margent. He had only arrived
the previous night, had at once visited the salon, and had
lost more than he cared to remember. He had never
played roulette before, but the proverbial luck of novices
had not favoured him, so that it was upon a temper of
which rage against luck, the bank, some disdain of
himself, and the incipient thirst of the gambler for more
play, that the contents of the telegram fell. Needless to
say that when he had read it the temper was, if possible,
a shade worse. For the moment he remembered only the
impossibility of getting his revenge from the bank if he
returned to London by the train leaving Nice that
forenoon. But it was for the moment only. Bob had been
spoilt somewhat by fortune. Never a reasonable wish, and
many an unreasonable one, of his but what had been
gratified by his indulgent parents. He was not so spoilt,
however, that it ever entered his head to disobey his
father's request. If the boy had nearly always got what he
wanted from his father or mother, they had got from him
in return what parents seldom seem to get now-a-days—
implicit obedience, the most ardent love, and the most
reverential worship. So it was that he did not stop to

reason whether he should go back or not. There was no "making up his mind," though he felt it a relief to curse the fates that drove him homeward so soon. One glance at the scene, a never-to-be-forgotten glance, a scene to constantly reappear, mirage-like, before his vision in the torturing days to come, then away. He wondered, half audibly, as he booked to Paris, whether he should not take a return-ticket—he had not intended to go back by way of Paris, and coming thence, had purchased a single ticket only—for he promised himself a speedy return.

Little he thought then that his farewell to Monte Carlo was the farewell to his care-free past, and the brightness and glory of existence! Some shadow of the future fell upon him, as, lying at his ease in the luxurious carriage, he re-perused the dispatch, and would not be removed. He noticed then, beneath the superfluous wording so foreign to the usual business-like brevity of his father's letters, the under-current of passionate entreaty, and blamed himself for his selfishness in not having seen it before.

"'Badly! life or death!' What does it all mean?" he pondered.

He could find no answer, cudgel his brains into even abnormal activity as he would. The gloom of the future rested on his spirit.

What the dispatch meant was clear enough to him, when, late in the afternoon of the second day from his departure from Nice, he walked into the principal's parlour of Messrs. Carlyon and Strathing, century-old bankers in Clement Lane. It meant ruin—and more than ruin—shame. He had left his father ten months before, apparently in the prime of life and the best of health, and good for another score years of a vigorous business career. He found him a half-palsied old man, with tottering feet and shaking hands, nerves that vibrated horribly at the slightest sound, and a piteous, oh, so piteous a look on his face, the look of the hunted.

"Father!" that was all that Bob could exclaim. The horror of his father's aspect struck at his heart, and for his very life he could not have uttered another syllable.

"Robert, at last you have come. I wanted you so badly—so badly."

It was the same phrase as that in the telegram. Bob felt rather than remembered this much.

"Why?" He did not mean to be abrupt, but the horror still held a vice-like grip of his pulses and his voice.

And then Bob saw what never passed with him into the oblivion of the forgotten.

With a shriek that rang through the cushioned panels of the private office, through the cashier's room, and into the outer counting-house—fortunately the clerks had all gone home—Strathing senior flung himself at the feet of his boy, and clasped his knees.

"Robert, my son, my son, save me!" This was what

the shriek carried to Bob's ears, from the poor gibbering lips, which had never previously spoken aught to him save in kindly raillery or loving counsel.

What mental power had not forsaken the younger Strathing he sent to recall a story he had once heard of the paralysis of limbs and brain which seized the Alpine guides when they observed the signs of the awful approach of an avalanche. For a moment as it actually was, for an eternity as it seemed, he could not think of his father—he could only think of the avalanche.

It was not strange that he should lose sight for that moment of his father's agony. The avalanche was falling upon him and those he loved, and intervened between his eyes and the prostrate, shrinking form of the old man.

But why detail all the mystery and the horror of the next few hours? We will put into a few sentences what the elder Strathing told his son, or rather what the son, when he had somewhat recovered from the shock, dragged from his father.

Carlyon and Strathing (that is to say Strathing, for Carlyon had long since passed into the region of the Shades) were on the eve of failure. The morrow might see their credit "blown upon," their "paper" returned and their shutters up. But the failure was the least of the trouble, bitter though it was. The collapse would be attributed, and rightly, to the fraud of the principal. Strathing senior was indeed in imminent danger of living the short years remaining to him in a felon's cell, and dying a felon. He had forged deeds, and stock, and merchandise warrants, and scrip transfers; he had appropriated trust moneys and deposits in the attempt to temporarily make good the deficiency in the bank's capital caused by loss on the Stock Exchange and irregular mining speculation. It was the old story told yet once again, this time with the difference, however, that it was not a trusted servant who was the defrauder, but the head of the firm.

Aroused cupidity, the brilliant prospects offered by an "unusually good thing," a loss, then further speculation to retrieve the damage only leading to other losses, the wrong act which was to operate for one day only and was to be corrected the next, the frantic struggling to keep the head above water as the speed of the infernal maelstrom increased—there is no need to recapitulate the characteristics of the perpetually recurring history. Suffice it to say that the ruin of Carlyon and Strathing appeared complete. Only one thing could avert it—the help of a certain old friend. But it was useless to expect his assistance if it were known that it was the "chief" himself that was guilty. Nor under any circumstances, to such a pass had the affairs of the bank been brought, would it be possible to prevent publicity being given to the peculiarity, not to say criminality, of some of the firm's late transactions.

This was, in effect, the revelation of the elder Strathing to the younger. This was the shameful ruin which Bob had read in his father's face on his entrance into the bank parlour.

When the whole story was out, sobbed forth by the wretched banker as he lay on the floor, for he could not get up, and Bob had to crouch beside him to listen, there was silence for a time in the fast-darkening room. The noise of the street traffic, never very loud in slow-going Clement Lane, was almost inaudible. The murmur somehow resolved itself into the plash of the Mediterranean wave on the Monte Carlo beach. The sea monody melted in its turn into the waltz strains rippling from the piano standing in the old drawing-room at Kensington, and Bob pulled his wits together just in time to save himself from falling into the unconsciousness which had already mercifully enwrapped the old man. The house-porter, a life-long dependent of the bank, came, and, wondering at the presence so long after hours of "the two masters," asked whether he should light the gas. No; no lights were wanted yet. Bob had loosened his father's old style neck-cloth, and had placed a sofa cushion under the grey head, and the old man's regular breathing indicated that he had passed from his faint into sleep. Bob would have liked the lights so as to have studied the old man's face; but he would not have them, because he did not care to see his own features, in the mirror which filled one of the wall panels. Poor fellow, he hated to learn the change which he felt had been wrought in him.

Years after, as old Pestle stood at the shaft's mouth, and reverently closed Bob's eyes, from which the life-light had vanished, he said—"When I first saw his eyes I felt that they had not been placed so. I believed they had been driven in by the awfulness of something that he had seen unexpectedly." Old Pestle was right, though there was nobody to tell him so. Bob's eyes were driven in that night by the dreadfulness of what he saw.

This is what he saw:—

His still loved and hitherto honoured father there prostrated, humiliated and disgraced. His darling mother—not as he had seen her last with her unbent form and hair unsilvered; her smile, that was unto those whom she cherished as a perpetual benison[6]—crushed, withered, shrinking, weeping for the grave in which to rest her suddenly whitened locks, before her time. One other woman, dearer perhaps than the one who bore him, though not yet nearer, whose placid face had shone always for him, with the serene purity of a love that had nothing, he used to fancy, earthly in it, stricken with the storm also, with her hopes wrecked and her happiness blasted. These figures he saw; the one in sad actualness of

---

[6] A blessing. (ed.)

place and time, the others in imagination scarcely less real. And himself—he feared to study the reflection of his features in the glass; but he did not spare his feelings as he gazed at his future. He realized that all was over in life for him; and the magnificent vistas opened before him by his education, by his social standing, and the position of junior partner in the bank, which in the course of the next year was to have been his, had been closed with an impenetrable seal. He saw himself at the threshold of his manhood burdened with a tainted name and carrying it through all the weary time.

No wedding now with the stately woman with the placid smile; he would be married to infamy "till death did them part."

For Bob had understood, without being expressly told so by his father, the thought in the latter's mind which had prompted the cry, "Save me, my son, save me!" His father had determined to make him the scapegoat for his crimes. His quasi-connection with the firm would enable this to be done readily. Two years before, immediately on leaving the University, Bob had taken a place in the bank counting-house, in order to obtain that practical insight into affairs necessary to qualify him for the assumption, sooner or later, of its management. He had proved himself to possess all the family aptitude for finance, and had shown such capacity that, towards the middle of the second year, his father had given him control of the stock and foreign loan transactions. Bob worked as few would have worked in his position. He took no advantage from his kinship with the "chief," and spared himself none of the routine drudgery. It was not so much a principle as a constitutional habit with him to do whatever fell to his hand with all his might. Thus it came about that at the close of his second year's probation, he knew as much of the intricate lore of the financial world as some men with ten times his experience. But his father had said that he was young enough to buckle on business harness, and had wished that he should spend a twelvemonth in travel before finally taking up his position in the bank.

Two months only of his holiday remained unexpired, when he had determined to run through Southern Europe, but he had got no further than the "hell" regions. He had seen "life" of course during his University terms and his travel. The world had left, however, few stains on his naturally strong and upright nature. He had backed a horse or two, and had gambled a little in other ways—we have seen him at Monte Carlo—but he had lost nothing he was not able to afford. With women he had always been tender and courteous and pure—the memory of the two women at home was a perfect Sir Galahad's shield to him always. He had helped many a friend and had deceived none. Picture yourself, then, as this young fellow, conscious of fair powers, conscious also of their limitations, perceiving countless opportunities for usefulness and honourable exertion, with an assured position in both the money-making and the money-spending worlds, and then picture yourself as him once more, when he realized that he was to be a perpetual bedfellow with shame. And if your self-portraiture be correctly drawn, you will, perhaps, taste a thousandth part of the agony that bit into Bob's heart and brain, and filled his veins as he sat there with the dreary nightfall closing upon him.

How long he sat, how long his father lay at his feet, how he got the old man—still unconscious—and himself into a cab, how they got home to Kensington, and at what hour, Bob never could remember. His perceptions revived only at the sound of his mother's voice.

"Robert, what does all this mean?" she wailed. "I have been nearly mad with the sense of ill, but he would tell me nothing, nor would he let me send for you. It is nothing that you have done, my boy, is it? Oh, say no!"

True and loyal soul, that for thirty years had believed she was possessed of the every thought of the bosom on which she nightly rested, it was not likely that she would ever doubt her husband. If trouble came, therefore, it must be through some one else, and the horrid fear had laid hold upon her that, from witnessing how her husband had withered under the blow, whatever it was, it must be connected with Bob. She strove to drive away the fearful suspicion, but it would not vanish. Her question, and the wholly eager, half suspicious glance that accompanied it, hurled upon her son the awfulness of his position. To give her the denial she craved, which his conscience warranted him in doing, would be really to thrust the ignominy of guilt upon his father. He would be the actual accuser of his father to his mother, for the old man had evidently not taken her into his confidence. To evade the question would be as bad as to reply in the affirmative, even if his mother would be content with less than a direct answer. And to say yes, while it might save his father, yet was it not to plant a fatal sting in the wounded mother's heart, and to do himself a vital injury? But if he was to do as his father wished, if he was to obey the unspoken command, "Yes," it must be, and "Yes" it was—not without a weak attempt at temporizing, however.

A doctor had been sent for, and had said that Mr. Strathing was in no danger, but had simply fainted.

"Wait till father comes to, mother darling, and I will tell you all."

"Robert, I must know now; Lois will watch your father."

And he then saw Lois for the first time. His father had been laid on a couch in the drawing-room, and by his head, bathing it with a cool lotion, stood stately Lois.

"Tell her all, Rob! You do not know how she has suffered these last days. Tell her all, and let her know the worst."

As Lois, the home-angel, as old Strathing had once called her, spoke, she did not lift her eyes, bent as they were in the performance of their tender task. Lois, as ever faithful to her own instincts and to her gracious training, put herself nowhere. She had suffered almost as acutely as Mrs. Strathing since the change in the banker's appearance and manner indicated calamity; but it was, "Tell her, for she has suffered," not "Tell us, for we have suffered."

Still Bob temporized—partly from the dread of the revelation, partly from the hope that his father would regain consciousness, and himself take up the miserable story.

"I have been travelling night and day, mother darling, since I got the dad's wire, and must have rest and food. I have eaten nothing today, I will tell you by and by."

"Robert," again spoke Lois. He started at the name; he had been "Rob" to her since the day when, fifteen years before, he had kissed her a boyish welcome to his home, which she had entered as a legacy—the only one the poor woman had to leave—to Mrs. Strathing from a widowed friend.

"Robert, your mother has scarcely touched food for three days, nor has she slept."

Bob now looked on his mother's face. He had purposely avoided doing so before. For half a century had time passed by, and left no finger-touch upon her cheek and forehead, fanned no devastating breath upon her hair. In all these years she had never been acquainted with personal sorrow. Ephemeral cares about her husband and son, or Lois, her adopted daughter, filled every niche of her heart not occupied by nearer ones; the troubles of her friends, or her dependents—these had been all her burdens.

But time had not forgotten, but had only postponed, the collection of the tribute of grief, which she, like every other creature of woman born, must pay him. In three days she had changed more in aspect than in all the blest years of her girlhood and wedded life. The suspense, the dread of she knew not what, which burdened her during that brief space had bleached her hair, and seared her brow and cheek. As Bob had seen her in his delirious gaze into the future in the bank parlour, so he saw her now—suddenly aged.

"God!" was the unexpressed prayer, "for one moment with Lois to tell which is best—kill my mother's hopes in me, or her wedded faith in father!"

God seemed silent then, as He did for many a day afterwards to all Bob's prayers, expressed and unexpressed. Lois still stooped over his father's form, and his mother stood before him waiting, waiting.

Yes, he would tell her; surely his father would right him with those dear ones, whatsoever he might let the outside world suspect. "Since you will have it so, mother and Lois, listen. The bank is on the point of failure, and I—I am to blame. I—" no, he could not say "robbed"—"I abused my trust." Had the words been those of confession, they could not have been spoken with more stricken pain. Bob did not recognize his own voice.

"Robert, my son, my son!" No accent of reproach in the mournful wail, no tinge of regret for the lost wealth; only measureless sorrow for the broken idol worshipped so devotedly by the mother and father, for the stricken ideals and the desolated hopes. Sick almost unto death as the young man felt, wrapped inextricably in the entanglements of the fate—woven net, he was glorified for the moment by the glimpse he got in that passionate exclamation of the heaven that awaited him when the great mother-love was informed of all. There was the utterest misery in her words then; there would be the fullest joy when she learnt the whole truth, even though the joy was bought at the sacrifice of faith in her husband. There was a reward there, at all events, for his present suffering.

And Lois? She was mute. She but bent the lower over the grey head on the couch-pillow, and stopped not in her loving ministrations. But she knew that she had received a blow beside which the grasp of death itself would have been welcome. The almost daily intimacy of the family circle in which Bob and Lois had grown up had not prevented the growth of the purest affection between them. As a boy, Bob had sworn fealty to her; through his youth and to the present time he had kept it; and but for this terrible thing, the "little wife" of his early days was to have become the wedded wife of his manhood. She had been his confidant always, his guide, she thought, always also. And this was what it had come to! Lois was no coward. Never a nobler or more courageous heart beat within womanly shape than hers, but she cried in the anguish of the sudden revelation that she might die then. She did not shrink from the overwhelming wave of trouble. She recoiled from the sin.

Only the stertorous breathing of the old man disturbed the stillness. Bob stood in the centre of the room when he had spoken. His mother had fallen coweringly into an easy-chair.

"Will you not speak to me, Lois?" at length asked Bob. He wanted her to look up, and hoped that she would read that in his gaze which might tell her something of the truth.

"Oh, Rob, what can I say? God help us all, you most of all!" Still she would not turn round.

"Then, you—" he would have added, "believe me guilty," but he stopped himself in time. Why should not she believe him? Had he not virtually confessed?

"Then, what? I do not understand," she said, having waited a moment for him to conclude.

"Then you have nothing to say to me. Have I already

fallen so low in your opinion as that?"

"Rob, you are unjust," she murmured in broken tones, raising her head now, but not venturing to glance at his face. "It is all so sudden—so awful. I have no time to think."

She had endeavoured to speak with her ordinary evenness of tone, but the effort was too much for her.

"Oh, Rob, my own love, how could you do it?" she cried between tearless sobs that rent her being. "How could you, when we all loved you so? We would have sacrificed our lives for you, everything to have prevented this wrong."

"And then—"

"But we do not love him less for this sin, do we, mother?"

From the depths of the chair there came a passionate echo—

"We do not love him less. More we could not have loved him. That is why it is so hard. Why did you do it, my son? If you had only trusted me!"

Once more Bob was nearly telling all. In the solitude of the bank parlour he had faced the consequences of taking upon himself the burden of shame. He had calculated upon meeting the scorn of some of his whilom companions, and the pity of others; he had tortured himself so far as to frame the words a judge would use in sentencing him, supposing he had to stand his trial, and was convicted; he had stung himself, too, with the fancied reproaches of those two loving women, but he had not bargained to suffer so much. Inconceivably more than the pain he had imagined was the reality. The grief of his mother and Lois filled his brain; his reason reeled under the injustice.

"Mother! Lois!" he cried, "have patience and you shall know everything. Do not judge me so hastily, for I am not—"

"Where am I? Robert, are you there?" came a feeble voice from the couch, just in time to remind Bob that he must say no more.

"You are at home, father, in the drawing-room. We are all here—mother, Lois, and I. You have been ill, taken with a fit or something of that sort, at the bank. Lie quiet, dear dad, and you will be better presently," and Bob, as he spoke, moved to his father's side, and took Lois' place. Mrs. Strathing rose from her chair, and also knelt by the old man, directing upon him a gaze in which nothing was visible but loving solicitude. What wonderful powers of repression some good women possess! A few moments before, and Mrs. Strathing's nature had undergone a momentous convulsion, but she showed nothing of its effects to her husband. In that supreme moment of wretchedness she could find no reason why she should deviate from her rule—to put her husband first, and herself last.

"Are you better, Edward?" she said, laying her hand on his brow. "Nay, dear, do not get up; you must not stir yet."

The old man had moved at her touch, and she thought he was attempting to rise. He meant, however, to turn his face to the wall. He could not meet her eyes, veiled as they were in a mist of tears. He made no response to her murmured inquiry. They believed that he had relapsed into unconsciousness. The seconds passed into minutes and the minutes into quarter hours before any one broke the oppressive silence.

"You have not dined, Robert, did you not say?" then questioned Mrs. Strathing. "You must not go longer without food."

Her voice seemed to rouse the banker. "I want to speak to Robert, he must not go away."

Mrs. Strathing feared that her husband's reproaches were about to burst on Bob. If she could only have known! With soothing words and caressing touch, she begged the old man to postpone what he had to say till his strength returned.

Without glancing at her, he motioned for her and Lois to go away, and for his son to come nearer. The ladies obeyed the gesture, and imagined that the banker still wished to save them from the knowledge of Bob's conduct.

"Robert," the old man whispered, clasping with his

weak arms his son's neck, so to bring the curly head close to the lips which trembled in the utterance, less from his powerlessness than his terror, "you have not told them?" The searching scrutiny of his father's look told Bob what he had not yet cared to admit to himself—that his mother and Lois were to be kept in ignorance, then and always, of the truth.

Bob, with his whole spirit revolting at the foulness of the wrong which was being done to him, could not answer him at once. His passion, scarcely held in check by his filial affection for his father, choked his speech. At last he found words. Freeing himself from the old man's hold, he said, "I have told them all!" For his life he could not help playing with his father's agony for that moment.

"All?" the old man groaned and shivered.

At the sound the ladies at the end of the room started forward.

Bob's natural greatness of heart spurred him to complete the sacrifice. "I mean, all that you would have them know—that the bank may fail, and that I have caused the smash," he hurriedly whispered.

Both Mrs. Strathing and Lois caught, and wondered at, the glance of gratitude the old man cast upon his son. They did not hear the half-inaudible exclamation—"It would kill Madeline to know all!" else they would have wondered the more. Long years afterwards they remembered the look—and then, when it was too late, remembered its significance.

"I will see you the first thing in the morning, father," said Bob. "You must not talk any more tonight." The banker acquiescing, Bob proceeded to his own room, faint in body, for he had fasted long, and was sick at heart. For the first time in his life beneath the home roof, he went to bed without his mother's kiss and the gentle pressure of Lois' hand.

The ladies busied themselves about the old man, and Bob would not make the first approach. He could not bear to have his customary caress received coldly, and he fancied that, as they believed him to be the one responsible for the present bitterness, they could not help but treat him with some severity. Poor Bob! How in his novitiate of suffering could he understand that both were hungering to enfold him in their arms, weep over him, and, it might be, purify his soul from the sin they suspected in him, by sweet drops from the chalice of their grief?

Sleep, calm and restful, did not abide with the Strathing family that night, nor, indeed, for many nights subsequently.

Scarcely had the day broke when the banker, weak and trembling, found himself in his son's room. Bob was waiting for him already dressed. The latter was the first to speak. He tried to make his words as tender as possible.

"There is no way out of this horrible mess then,

father, but that I must bear the brunt of these—blunders?"

"Let us be frank, Robert, now. If I had been frank before there would have been no trouble. God forgive me. When you said blunders, you meant crimes. Call them so."

The banker spoke in the quavering accents of a coward.

"Let that pass, sir," and Bob, as he replied, felt springing up within him a contempt for his father which lent a sting to his next words. "We have no time to lose. If I am to figure as a criminal, it is just as well I should begin to study the part."

"For your mother's sake, Robert, spare me, though I deserve all."

"You said you wanted us to be frank with one another, sir. You can hardly expect me to take up willingly this load of disgrace. But I will say no more—for the sake of her you have just invoked. It is for her I do it all." And then his mood changed, and the remembrance of his father's countless past kindnesses rose up before him.

"No, I don't mean that, father. I would do it for you as well, for everything I have and am came from you, and is yours if you want it. But it is very hard, father, very hard, and you will not let me tell even Lois. This is the cruellest of all—that my mother and Lois should misjudge me."

"Boy, boy, every word you say is a knife thrust into my heart. But if you tell Lois she will not let your mother remain ignorant. She has only the attachment of an affectionate friend for me, for your mother she has the devotion of a daughter, and to you she bears all the love of a wife. She will not let you, her almost husband, be wrongfully blamed by your mother. She will not allow a shadow to remain between the two people she loves best on earth."

"You forget, father, that Lois owes you everything, and you are not right in saying she regards you merely as a friend. She has for you all the fondness of a daughter. Let me tell Lois."

"To tell Lois, I say, will be to tell your mother. Rather than that the whole world shall know. It is bad enough for your mother to think you are to blame. All night long she has been tossing on her bed crying 'My son! my son!' But for her to learn that I am the cause!" The old man in his terror and remorse became inarticulate.

"Be it so, then, sir." Bob's voice again unconsciously assumed severity of tone, and he could not use the "father." "I am to suffer to the bitter end. I have to face the world as guilty. That I will do. I have to face mother and Lois as guilty. That I must do. But I can never marry Lois while this stigma clings to me. Never to be righted. Oh, my God!"

"I will right you, Robert—when I get into smooth

waters again—at least with your mother and our dear girl." With the readiness of the weak drowning in the waters of disaster to grasp anything promising safety, the banker seized and flung this straw of consolation to his son.

"How could you do that? It would but add to the shock to know that you had consented to my bearing the consequences of the wrong. Lois might be told perhaps, but never mother, and then only in case mother died. But tell me what has to be done. If the bank has to be saved I must know how."

We need not follow Strathing senior and junior in their conference. As it proceeded the younger man saw that it would be only too easy a matter for him to appear as the perpetrator of the fraudulent acts. The fatal bonds adapted themselves with facility to his form. His functions during the major portion of his two years of bank service dove-tailed as it were into the frauds with fearful accuracy. So apparent indeed was the precision with which the frauds could be adjusted to his work, that more than once the suspicion arose in his mind that in all his bank labours his father had used him as his tool. In this he was wrong. It was in fact that very circumstance which first suggested to the banker the idea that he might save himself and the bank by placing shameful responsibility on the shoulders of his son. He said as much to Bob, and in such a way that the young man did his wretched parent the justice of believing him.

Had it been clear to him that the banker had used his integrity, his innocence of the world, and his relationship as so many factors in his fraudulent calculations, the young man's love for his father would have been utterly destroyed, and with it would have gone most of that faith in God and man which proved his salvation in the dark hours to come.

As Bob was "to bear the brunt," so had he, in that conversation between himself and his father, to do all the thinking. All the subsequent actions, too, would have fallen to his lot had it been possible. The elder Strathing was one of those slender-fibred men who neither bend nor break before the storms of adversity, but who are simply laid low and crushed to the verge of annihilation. He had been intellectually flattened out by the disaster that menaced his position in the world. The powers of the intellect and the financial grasp which had enabled him so to deal with securities as to make the "Strathing frauds" notorious on the Stock Exchange as models of nefarious cunning and perverted ingenuity had vanished in the intensity of his dread.

The result of the deliberations between father and son was that application was made to the former's old friend for a sufficient sum to meet the most pressing claims and to release the minor forged or misapplied securities. To obtain the money, as no security could be given by the firm, and the amount was lent from motives of pure friendship, it was necessary to furnish the lender with a statement of the bank's accounts. It was the wretched task of the old man to do this. He had then to pose as the accuser of his son as the one guilty of the frauds which had shaken the old house of Carlyon and Strathing to the foundations.

As it was tolerably clear that, given time and adherence to the beaten paths of finance, the firm would reach solvency again, the money was got.

Not so easily satisfied were the claims of the holders of the valueless bonds and deeds representing large amounts. These were for the most part firms in the first rank of financial magnates, who would sooner lose a few thousands than allow a forger or manipulator of securities to go unexposed and unpunished. The suspicions of more than one of them as to the validity of some of the documents held to cover advances to the Strathings were roused, and inquiries at the brokers and the Stock Exchange were not as a rule reassuring. In several cases where loans had to be renewed an extension of time was not procurable till Mr. Strathing confessed that the securities were forged and asserted that the criminal was his son. A prosecution was only averted from pity for the father. Heinous as was the banker's sin, it was bitterly punished by the torture to which he was subjected in making these false confessions, and in listening, he, the real offender, to the commiserations lavished upon him because of the actions of his unworthy offspring.

Again and again would the old man have told the whole truth but for the recollection of his wife. Though legal process was not taken against Bob, there were few people in financial circles who were not aware of the serious accusations levelled against him; bank walls have ears, and repeat what they hear sometimes, and the tongues of bank and brokers' clerks will wag. To the bank, hitherto of unimpeachable credit, many a kindly act was tendered when it leaked out that only time was requisite for it to pull through the crisis. For the old man and the family, unlimited sympathy, as genuine as boundless, but for Bob only merciless contempt and scorn. To his own intimates he was the most corrupt of whitened sepulchres, and "with such a father, such a mother, such a woman for his betrothed, and such prospects, to do this! Faugh!" For the persons who knew him slightly or not at all, it was the cause of much righteous indignation that the authorities had been so culpable as not to call him to account. It would have been a mercy to his parents to have locked him up for fourteen years at Portland, to say nothing of the relief to society. True, there was pity for Bob outside of his home, but it was confined to the clerks and the other servants of the bank. They did not suspect the father, but they could not bring themselves to suspect the son, much less find him guilty. For he had worked with them side by side, and there was not one of them but whose work when in arrears he had helped to perform. Not one but who had felt all the better for his kindly words and cheery laugh. But their opinion didn't count.

And Bob? During the progress of the negotiations for settling the affairs of the bank, he had remained at home, going out at night only to the bank to help his father there, or for a stroll for health's sake. His was the controlling will while the whole dreary business was afoot. He guided his father's actions, prompted him here, and checked him there, so as to secure coherency between the facts as they were and what had to be shown as facts to others. It was well for him that the task was so great as to demand his utmost energies. He was left no time to brood. In his leisure he prepared himself resolutely, so far as he could do mentally, to meet the altered world. Very altered was it to him. He had insisted upon his father telling him what people said; he had done the same with the old confidential clerk and cashier, with whom he had to hold many conferences—so that he knew well how he was regarded. Altered particularly to him was the spot which had been his world—his home. His mother and Lois were still affectionate and tender towards him, but there was a change. They thought it was in him, he thought it was in them. He saw them seldom, his meals were served in his own rooms. Once his mother had tried to gain his confidence, but there could be no confidence given because of the wall erected between them by his father's appeal. Then the poor woman sought Lois' aid, though she writhed at the need of the help of another to unlock her boy's heart. But Lois was no more successful. She conjured him by his love for her, by the memory of their youth and their early friendship, to treat her again as his old-time confidant. He was kind but he was resolute. He would tell her nothing. The dear women had bewailed to the banker their failure. How he suffered as they told him! They besought him in his daily consultations with Bob, to beg him to be frank and open with them. As to the actual details they knew next to nothing. They understood more or less vaguely that somehow Bob had robbed the bank, and had all but caused its collapse, but that was all. Why he had done so, they did not know, could not imagine. "Could it be caused by gambling debts?" questioned the mother of the banker. "Was it not at Monte Carlo your message found him?" Her husband dare not trust himself to reply; he could only shake his head. Others outside, who were curious to know what the young fellow had done with the money, were quite sure it was gambling that had ruined Strathing junior. The few hours and the few rouleaux he had spent at Monte Carlo were respectively magnified a thousandfold. If his first game at roulette had not played havoc with Bob's purse, it had put the finishing touch to his reputation.

When all was settled, when the last forged deed and scrip had been redeemed, and the last penny of the misappropriated trust moneys replaced, and the apparently uninjured craft of Carlyon and Strathing's bank in a fair way to reach the haven of financial security, Bob told his father he had determined to go to Australia. The gold-diggings, though nearly ten years had elapsed since their discovery, were still always in men's minds, and Bob considered he might as well go there as anywhere. His decision surprised and shocked the banker. In the midst of the complications from which his son had freed him, he had never bestowed a thought on that son's future.

"You must not go away, Robert," he exclaimed. "What will become of the bank supposing I take ill or die? I am not the man I was before this trouble—before I did so wrong."

Mr. Strathing was very humble now. Unlike most sinners, once the fear of a dread penalty was removed, he did not forget his offence. He was morbidly sensitive to it when by himself or with Bob; hence the amendment of his phrase. He feared to speak of his wrong-doing too generally or impersonally.

"What good can I do by staying?" was his son's rejoinder. "I can't go to the bank, my presence would injure it. You must take a partner; his money will free you from your liability to Wilson; why not take Wilson's son in?" Mr. Wilson was the name of the old friend of Mr. Strathing who had advanced him the large sum without security. "He is young and able, and will soon pick up the running."

"I had never dreamt of this," continued the old man. "I had thought that after a time you would have taken your place in the bank as if nothing had happened."

"Sir, don't talk in this way, to other business men, I mean; I say it with all respect. If you do, they will suspect that the blow has weakened your judgment permanently. You must know how such an impression would damage the bank."

There was a pause, and then Bob resumed passionately—

"Besides, father,"—the banker's eyes dimmed over, the young man had for the first time since the interview in the bedroom so addressed him—"I could not stand it. Let me think of myself now a little. I have considered you up to the present. Imagine what it would be for me to be seen about the city, pointed at, sneered at, congratulated perhaps on my narrow escape from a felon's cell."

"Robert, you are merciless, but I deserve it all."

"Nay, father, I did not mean to be unkind. I did not measure my words, and I beg your pardon."

"That is worse than all; it is I that should beg your pardon hourly, momentarily."

"Enough of this, father! You will see I cannot stop here."

"But your mother and Lois! They cannot bear the separation."

"Are we not separated now, as far as the Poles, because—you will make me speak against my will, when my words must be so many daggerstabs in your heart."

"Never mind me, my son, it is but just punishment."

"God knows, I have no wish to punish you. All I say is, that because my words give you pain is another reason for my going. For me to stay would be for you to have a thorn constantly in your side. I must go. Will you tell mother and Lois?"

"If you say I must, I will do so," murmured, in broken tones, the heart-wrung old man.

"And you must tell Lois, too, that I give her back her freedom." The poor fellow had steeled himself to tell this to herself, but his courage had failed him.

"Oh, Robert, there is no need for that. Lois loves you as ever—nay, with a deeper love if possible."

"I shall never marry. I would have none but Lois, and Lois would not have me as I am."

"Have you as you are? No woman alive is worthy of you as you are, Robert; and of all women unmarried Lois is the worthiest." The banker had told Bob he was merciless; he was merciless to himself as he continued—

"Lois would take you as you seem, and then when the

moment comes when I can right you, think of the worship and the adoration that will be yours."

"We have discussed this point before, father, and uselessly. Lois must not be told till mother is dead, and pray heaven she may live for twenty years yet. I will not marry Lois till I am cleared, and we must not ask her to wait without knowing for what till the best years of her life are past. She must be—she shall be free!"

Decisively as Bob pronounced the words, his form shook with noiseless sobs. His father was even more stirred by the violence of his emotion.

"The *Champion of the Seas* sails for Melbourne in a week, father. I shall leave by her. Will you tell mother at once, please?"

"I will if you insist, Robert. You have the right to command now, my place is to obey," answered Mr. Strathing sadly.

He did as he promised. Heaviest of all the strokes that had yet fallen on him was his wife's tearless grief when he communicated their son's resolve to her. She had aged greatly these latter weeks, but this last announcement transformed her into an old woman.

As for Lois, when the banker told her what Bob had said, she made no response, but received the news so apathetically that the old man wondered whether the desolation of spirit had not previously reached its extreme. He had determined in his own mind to beg her to refuse the offered release from her betrothal vow. When the time came, however, he was powerless to put his entreaty into words. And it was as well for his own sake that he was incapacitated. So close were the girl's tears to the surface, so near to overflowing the pent-up forces of her violated hopes and disappointed love, that at another word she would have broken down utterly. The old man's burden would have been too heavy to have been borne, had he witnessed her agony. Shattered himself beyond further endurance, he could not have helped but tell her all, and that her hero, her Bob, was as pure and strong as she had once dreamed him.

Neither Mrs. Strathing nor Lois attempted to persuade their dear lad, never so dear as now, from carrying out his intention. They were in doubt whether he was not acting wisely after all. On the ground of health alone, his decision seemed best. His strength had gone; his physique modified; while his face, so changed had it become, might have been ravaged by a decade of disease. In any case, the barrier between them seemed to grow higher as the day of departure drew nearer. They said little to one another of the impending step and less to Robert. But all their waking moments—and they gave few to sleep that week—were spent in his service, preparing for his departure, weaving in with their work myriad prayers, and sanctifying their work with the blessed incense of their sighs and tears.

The night before Bob's departure arrived. Happy the family that in its homely annals knows not such experience as the last night before the change in the old order of domestic things.

The last dinner together was a very quiet one. Only, towards the end Bob said with his old tenderness of intonation, "Mother darling, a few words with you in your own room?"

"My boy, yes!" All the wrung mother's heart went forth to him in the simple phrase.

"Lois, dear—after mother?" As he spoke he put all his fearless frankness, latterly hidden under compulsion, into the gaze with which he sought his erstwhile sweetheart's face. She dared not return the look as she motioned assent.

In the life of every human being there are arcana that may not be unveiled, experiences that may not be narrated. There were in that last interview between Mrs. Strathing and her son such unrevealable mysteries. There was the mother moaning with instinctive rebellion against the loss of her boy, fearing to keep him, yet still more fearing to separate from him; all her faculties clouded with the horrid misapprehension as to the young man's guilt, hating to reproach him, but craving with a longing the intensest to beg him to walk so in the future that neither God nor man should find aught to censure in him. There was the son, rocked with tumultuous passions to which, if he is not to plant deeper stings than those he plucks out, he must not give expression, bleeding inwardly from the wound his mother unconsciously dealt him by her every word and gesture, yet not daring to raise his voice in vindication, suffering the more because with respect to himself alone the acuteness of her sorrow was so unnecessary. And over them both, bearing them down, accentuating with despair every syllable and caressing movement, the certainty—derived whence they knew not—that when they parted they would never meet on earth again. When Bob at last wrenched himself from his mother's arms, he left her fainting on the couch. It was with salt drops blinding his vision that he sought Lois.

He found her in the garden. The Strathings' house stood in the midst of its own grounds, small in area, but fertile in the beauty which still clings to many homes in the Old Court suburb. It was a moonlight night in June. One of the poet's "rare days," when "Heaven tries the earth, if it be in tune, And over it softly her warm ear lays," had been succeeded by an equally perfect night. A vagrant breeze, in which lingered a reminiscence of the day's heat, now and then stirred the sleeping flowers, whispered cooingly through the streets, and irresolutely dallied with the creepers mantling the walls. The rustle of the leaves as the tiny breath played with them was the only sound distinctly audible. Nature preached peace, and Lois, as she stood in the centre of the oval lawn, whereon the moon had showered her most brilliant light till it resembled the argillaceous shield of some giant knight, wondered why men could work such wrong as to dull their ears to so gracious a sermon. It was a scene for lovers to confess mutual love, and to murmur vows—not for the indulgence of protests against the devastating fates, that, breaking hearts, yet compels them to continue their pulsing.

"Lois," said Bob softly, so as not to startle her, "shall we speak here? No one can overhear us, and I would like our last talk to take place where we have held so many sweet ones." He had not intended to make so tender a reference to the past, but the charm of the night betrayed him.

"I had the same thought, Rob," replied Lois, in quiet tones, the tremulousness of which was barely perceptible even to Bob's intent hearing.

The young man looked at her with the dreamy light enwrapping, as with a filmy garment, her statuesque beauty. He drank in with his glance the sweet stillness of her eyes, and the refined grace of her features. He thought he had never seen her appear so beautiful, and yet he was to lose her for always. He had not ventured to take her hand.

"Lois, you have been dwelling upon the delightful past? Forgive me, dear, for alluding to these times, but I must in this—last hour."

He faltered, but forced himself to continue—

"Why I do so is to say this, that whatever you may think me now, I was then, if not worthy of you—no one could be that, I, perhaps, less than most—but at all events not absolutely unworthy of you. Believe that of me always, will you?"

This was more than the girl could bear.

"Rob," she cried, burying her face in her hands, "if I think of those days, don't let us talk of them. Let the past be dead, dear, if not to speech, to memory. Let us talk of the future. But I will think of you as you were when you first came from college—if I can."

Her honest soul would not let her withhold the final words, but as she had unconsciously lowered her voice, they passed unheard by Bob.

"Ah, Lois! I shall be the better for all the rest of my days for knowing that. And now, dear, for my future."

He tried to be cheerful as he spoke, but miserably failed.

"Father gave you my message?" he at length asked.

"Oh, Rob!" the words struggled through a storm of weeping, "that must not be, unless—" She could not end the sentence.

"Unless what, Lois? Nay, never mind. You must be free. You could never marry a man upon whom so foul a stain rests."

"Is it that you do not care for me, or care for me less, Rob?"

"Before heaven, no! I have no right now to say one word of love to you, other than what I might utter to a sister, perhaps not that—but—but, if you could only read my heart!"

"Then I shall not give you back your promise. I shall look upon you always as my affianced husband."

Never before did the deep liquidity of her voice move Bob as it did now.

"I cannot accept the sacrifice, Lois—noble Lois. I should be an utter wretch to refuse you your freedom."

"I will not have it, Rob!" And with a gesture full of delicacy, as if she were giving him back some rare thing he had offered her, she placed her hands on his breast.

"I will never give you up—never!" she repeated; "as you were my first, you shall be my only love."

The young man shook at her touch. Seizing her hand, he exclaimed—

"But, Lois,"—there was a deep pathos in his accents—"have you considered what it would mean, supposing I came back for you some time hence? Do you realize what it would be to have others always thinking of the stain on your husband's life, to have them distrusting him and commiserating you? Think of the torture, of the burning pain, for which there would be no cure!"

"Yes, there would be a cure," she murmured softly,

the passion of her love, which had put a fierce energy into her previous words, having lost its fire for the moment. "I would surely find it in your love, and in the growing strength of your character, I will not give you up, because I want you to be strong, Rob. I hope and believe that from the fiery furnace of this trial you will come out purified and strengthened; and, Rob,"—never, while he drew breath, did he forget the ineffable delicacy with which she murmured her next words—"a wife who knows both your strength and your weakness will help you as no one else can."

Before he could find speech she began again—

"Am I not bold, Rob? It is because I, we all, love you, know that you can do so much more in life, if you will, and—and—we fear that, unless you keep all the old ties unbroken, you may—grow careless."

Bob understood. They, his mother and Lois, suspected he might fall into evil, fresh evil as they thought, or into the recklessness which is too often worse than positive evil, for in it are all the germs of consummate wickedness. For a minute he was revengeful and angry. Then, the tempest passed, and he disdained himself for his weakness, as he termed it. Did he need further schooling to play his part well? Had he graduated in suffering, only to find that he could not listen in patience to noble words, because they were inspired by an erroneous belief for which he himself had besought credence? As he reflected, Lois, always the best and purest of women to him, grew in moral stature.

When he opened his lips the next time, his words were humble and broken. "I accept the sacrifice, Lois," he said, "but I shall never be worthy of you. A man unstained by—crime—would not be, and how can I ever become so? But never fear that I shall do serious wrong again." He half-smiled as he noticed how aptly he was employing phrases and tones in keeping with his part of the sinner in the sad tragedy in which they all were actors. Continuing—

"With God's help, and He will grant me that if I have your and darling mother's prayers, you will never have need to blush for me again."

She flung herself on his breast in passionate tears. He scarcely recognized his dignified Lois, in the clasping, weeping woman.

"Rob, my darling, be good, be strong. Our prayers will be always with you and following you. We will forget all, except that you are working for the crown of a great redemption. You will come back to us, and you will then—marry me, Rob" (this with a sweet shyness), "and we will be all happy once more."

The presentiment that he would never return was strong upon him, but he had not courage to tell her so. He would say nothing to damp her newly-awakened hope in him.

"Rob," said Lois, after she had found her voice again, "will you make me a promise?"

"A thousand, if you wish it, dearest Lois. My whole life is yours henceforth—every moment of time, every impulse, every faculty."

"Nay, Rob, I only ask one great thing. I fear to pain you, dear, but I must say it."

"Speak out, Lois, do not hesitate. You have given me so much in giving me yourself, that nothing I can do will ever reach a thousandth part of its equivalent."

"Then, it is this. I do not ask what amount the bank lost—through you, but it must have been very large."

He interrupted her. "Very large," he said quickly.

"I feared so," was the response. "That makes the task the more terrible, but the victory will be all the greater. I wish you, Rob, to send home to the bank every penny of your earnings, be they little or be they much, in liquidation of the debt. You may make your fortune suddenly—others have done so across the seas, have they not?—but I do not count on that, nor must you. Stint yourself of everything except the meagrest necessaries of life and health, economize to the uttermost fraction, and send all your savings home regularly."

Thrilled by the girl's noble earnestness, Bob could not smile at what he deemed to be her lack of worldly knowledge, though tempted to do so.

"At such work as I shall be fit for out there, my savings

in twenty years would not clear the debt," he said.

"I do not suppose they would," she replied. "It is not so much for the sake of the bank, Rob, that I want your promise, but for your own."

"I scarcely understand, Lois. Would it not be best for me to let my savings accumulate there, where, if I saw a suitable opening for profitably using them, I would have them at command. In the colonies there must be plenty of such openings, and, by taking advantage of one or other of them, I might be in a position to sooner repay the bank."

"No, you do not understand me, Rob. After all, the money you—I mean what the bank lost—would have been yours in time, and it is not the debt I am anxious about. I am anxious only for you. If you resolve to lay aside—week by week, or month by month, for remittance home—all except your bare living expenses, you will have a definite aim before you. Every effort of exertion, every stroke of the pen, every drop of sweat, every minute spent in labour, every penny saved and gained, will be so many tokens of victory over your dead self, and so many stones in building up the new Robert Strathing." In the pleading of her love, in the justification of her love to herself, Lois became eloquent. She lifted up her face to her lover's. Her words were not more intense than the earnest appeal in her features. As he was about to speak she placed a finger on his lips.

"One more word, Rob. I propose this course not as a penance nor as a punishment. Your sufferings in the present, and what you will have to suffer in the tearing asunder of the old relations will be surely accepted by Heaven as atonement. But it is a means of purification, of regeneration. My darling," she concluded with a passionate cadence, "if I were in your place I would live on half-a-crown a week, if at all possible, to do this."

Strangely moved, Bob said—"I believe you would, my Lois; and with Heaven's aid I will do so too. I will make you the promise."

"That is my Rob," Lois returned. "But I do not ask you to keep the promise always. Keep it for five years. Few men will be stronger, few purer, dear. Then come and claim me. I will never blush for you. Few will have the right to reproach you, and what if they choose to exercise it? I shall be at your side. The bank will give us enough to live upon, even though you take no part in its business."

And so the curious compact was arranged. The savour of the kiss that sealed it never departed from Bob. It was to his imagination more than the confirmation of a vow. It was a consecration to the noblest life which, stigmatized as he was, was possible to him. From the moment Lois' lips touched his, the horror of his father's cruelty in thus condemning him to obloquy which frequently surged like a destructive wave through his consciousness, lost its power. The feeling of rebellion did not die at once—did not even perceptibly lose its grip on him at once. Slowly and surely, however, it evaporated, and in its stead arose an ardent desire to attain that pinnacle of manliness, the point where self dies utterly, its vitality extinguished in the rarefied atmosphere of the table-lands "to which our God Himself is sun and moon."

One other interview had Bob that night with his father. Here, the younger was the exhorter, the counsellor, and the director. The elder Strathing said little. If ever remorse and humiliation held possession of a human soul, they reigned supreme in the old man's bosom in that bitter hour. The burden of his cry was: "I will right you, my son, as soon as I dare, with Lois; immediately if anything happens to your mother." He had taken care, he further said, "to prepare such documents that in the event of his death justice should at once be done to his son, so far as could be possible, without injury to the bank."

The next morning Bob took train for Liverpool, whence the *Champion of the Seas* was to set sail.

Mr. and Mrs. Strathing and Lois went with him. Erring as she believed her boy to have been, feeble as she herself had become, the elder lady could not deny herself the sad pleasure of being with him to the last. The final good-byes were spoken just before the tug cast off the good ship in the Mersey estuary. His father clasped Bob's hands with a fervent: "God bless you always, dear lad;

you are a hero!" Lois, as she kissed him, murmured—
"Sweet, the promise; remember the half-crown;" hiding
her emotion beneath a brave mask of smiles. But Mrs.
Strathing could only press him convulsively to her. Her
voice failed her, and her love and her fears found
expression in precious tears—the words of dumb, pangful
souls.

Three months afterwards, in the latter days of '59, the
Champion of the Seas anchored in Hobson's Bay.

Amongst the hundred and fifty passengers whom
good Captain Outridge landed on the shores of the new
land was Robert Strathing. He had resolved, come what
might, he would not change his name. He would take no
alias; but he had also resolved that where not absolutely
necessary he would not disclose it. It was possible that
some knowledge of the Strathing frauds might have
reached the colony. The filaments of finance ramify in all
directions, and he had no wish to unnecessarily erect any
barrier in his own path. On board ship the blunder of a
partially deaf purser had given him the choice of several
cognomens—none correct. He had answered to Athing,
Stathing, Ring, King, and even Thing indiscriminately.
His letters he ordered to be detained in the Melbourne
office till he sent for them.

Once on shore, Bob, like most new chums, decided
to experiment in digging. He had brought some money
with him, and this and spasmodic luck carried him

through several fields and rushes till he found himself on the Pleasant Creek. He had several mates—mostly "new chums"—of more or less gentle descent—some, like himself, with a history. It was to one of these latter, at one of his earliest "camps," that in response to a remark as to the rigid economy, almost parsimony, of his personal expenditure, he said—"If I could live upon half-a-crown a week, I would do it." The words had slipped out half unconsciously, for Bob was dreaming of home. His chum laughed, and he repeated the remark that not one miner in a thousand could live upon half-a-crown a day in those times, when for the commonest necessaries famine prices had frequently to be paid. Bob was never able to make Lois' half-crown suffice for a week. When he got to the Creek home, he brought his expenses so low as to come within measurable distance of the sum. It was due to accident; this he candidly confessed to Lois in one of his monthly letters. If he had not chanced to hear old Carl Groth, the German butcher, lament that he could not get any one to put his books in order, he would not have had the opportunity of offering to drop into the shop once a week to square them. Nor, but for the same accident would Osborne, the general storekeeper, have heard of his accountancy abilities, and have begged him to do the like favour for the store-books. From neither of these good fellows would he receive payment, except in kind, though he saved them more in a week than he earned in a month by his pick. He supplied his own modest wants, and occasionally requisitioned on one or the other for goods to meet a case of want. But that was all. He would assist Pestle, too, with his registers if they got in arrears, and as he did not care to pay himself out of Pestle's stock of drugs (holding what that gentleman considered to be the very heterodox view that a blue pill was in no sense life-sustaining, and a black draught not particularly useful as a body covering), he did not hesitate to accept remuneration in the shape of lent volumes. By the help of these accessories Lois' ideal of economy was nearly attained, and month by month remittances went homewards, old Pestle and Pestle's Melbourne correspondent being agent for the transmission, for Bob, ever sensitive to the shadow resting on his name, and wishful of avoiding the semi-publicity of the Post-office, had begged the chemist's permission thus to make use of them.

THE LETTER

"TO EDWARD STRATHING, ESQ..
Banker.
Clement's Lane, London, E.C.

Pleasant Creek, Victoria.
December 28, 1862.

"MY DEAR SIR.

"The black border of the envelope which covers this will have perhaps already told you of the sad, the awful news I have to communicate. Without preamble, I must inform you that your son, dear Robert Strathing, died in my arms on Christmas Eve, and was buried today. I tell you the fact boldly, and do not wrap it up, as perhaps I might have done, in roundabout phrases. For I take it, sir, that you are a man. Only a man, a brave and strong man, could have had such a glorious son. 'Like father, like son,' they say, and it must, it must have been so in your case, and poor 'Half-Crown.' (Pardon me, it's the name we oftenest called him, and always spoke of him by—why, I will tell you later on, for it's not one of the things, I should say, that the dear lad would tell you himself). It is because I think you such a man that would prefer to take the whole force of the blow at once, rather than in instalments, that I say at the outset, 'Your son is dead!' That this news will be a heavy blow, no one that knew him can doubt. Here, he was idolized—I am not given to the habitual use of strong expressions—and yet we saw only half, perhaps not that much, of his nature. To those who saw him as he really was, in his complete manhood, what must his death be? I don't care much for poetry, but here and there a line has fixed itself in my memory. Some one—I think it was Shakespeare—has spoken of 'a loss darkening the world.' The loss of Bob has darkened our world for us. I fear me that our eclipse is as sunlight to the gloom which will overtake you and your family. Your sorrow will be so great that sympathy from us out here will be intrusive. Therefore, I hold my peace.

"I will tell you how he died. He died, as I fancy—'tis only my fancy—he had lived, a hero. It was on the afternoon the day before Christmas. Bob had 'knocked off' (our colonialism for stopped work) earlier than usual. He had done so to give the people on the Creek a treat. It's a long story to tell, but I had better go through with it, so that you may understand every detail about his last hours. You would never guess what the treat was. It was such a simple thing, and nobody on the diggings except your son would have thought of it. He had the knack of making simple deeds gracious and sweet, while other men would have only made themselves ridiculous. Only that day Bob had received by post from a Tasmanian lad a queer-looking parcel. When he opened it, he found it was a box containing three sprigs of English holly with the berries on. He had not had half-a-dozen words with the young fellow, when he was on the field, but, like everybody else, he swore by Bob. He had got tired of digging, and had gone home to his people in Launceston a few weeks before. He had heard, by chance, of a holly tree at New Norfolk, right the other end of the island, and that the tree had retained its berries up to that time. Off he went by coach, travelled the hundred and fifty miles there, begged a piece of the holly, was refused, then stole several bits, the best on the tree, he wrote, with the ripest berries on, returned to Launceston, and sent the sprigs to Bob as a Christmas gift. The lad didn't know Bob's name, but he addressed the packet to 'Old Half-Crown, Pleasant Creek.' He was certain it would find its destination, and sure enough it did. As a colonial, the young fellow could only imagine, not realize, what those pieces of holly meant to Bob, and to lots of other Englishmen on the fields. While the youngster had lived in the camp, he had generally gone by the name of the 'Whelp,' and had been cursed indefinitely by every party he had worked with, but every British soul on that Christmas Eve blessed him heartily. Well, as I was saying, Bob was resolved to give the people a treat. There are people from every clime under the sun here; but sons of the old land are in the majority, and you will understand—no, I don't see, on second thoughts, how you will understand—how they would welcome a sight of holly berries on Christmas Eve. But nobody but Bob would have thought of giving them that sight, of sharing his rare pleasure with them. That was his treat—he took the holly in his hands, and he went nearly all over the field with it. How the news spread; how women wept, and men too; how everybody remembered the old mother-land, though a cruel stepmother she had been to some of them; how many kissed the berries! Yes, kissed them; how some tried to grab them (colonialism again, sir), and how a big fellow from Yorkshire, and not long out, clutched one of the sprigs, and was knocked down for his pains (not by Bob)—how all this happened I have not space to tell. It did happen; and foolish as an account of it might appear in the Times, yet the effect of it wasn't foolish, by any means. Everybody felt happier, more Christmas-like, for that little lot of holly. And it was all Bob's idea and that young Tasmanian's. To get on with my sorrowful story—Bob, who had started from the west of the camp, had reached the eastern, the reefs or township part, on his march with the holly, and had just reached my shop and said, in his own bright way—'Here, Pestle, here's something for you, old man! Keep it quiet, or else you'll be burnt out tonight. I've been nearly mobbed getting this far.' I looked up from my registers (he used to help me with them sometimes), and saw he was offering me a piece of holly. Or rather, I thought I saw, for I could not really trust my eyes or my luck. To think of holly with the berries on at Christmastide! I'm a Quaker—perhaps I'd better say I was—and don't care a button for Christmas ceremonies. But the holly was different. I went the length of my shop in one bound and grasped the sprig. If it had not been real, but only imitation, I believe I should have struck Bob, even though it was Bob. He let me have it, and was clearing away without thanks, just like his dear modest self, when, my eyes having got better—somehow they had dimmed for the moment—I said, 'Look here, Half-Crown, come to dinner to-morrow. I've often asked you and you would never accept. Do come, for the sake of Christmas and the holly!' He paused for a moment at the door, and then smiling, replied—'Well, I'll come, and the hospital can have the piece I was keeping for myself.' I saw then that he had two other pieces of the shrub in his hand. 'Thanks, Half-Crown, you're a good fellow to consent at last,' I said, and asked him what he was going to do with the last bit. I found he intended it for Mrs. Hamilton. She is our new doctor's wife—made a bad match of it, poor lady, but stuck to her husband through all this strange goldfield life. Bob, for a wonder, had never spoken to her, but he knew instinctively how she would appreciate the gift; so he asked me to send it to her. I promised, of course, and he turned to go in the direction of the hospital, saying as he went out, 'It will be good medicine for them, poor lads!'

"Those were his words as he passed to his death. Always for others was Bob, always.

"He had not gone ten yards from my door when a miner came rushing down the hill, crying—'Campbell's has fallen in, and some of the fellows are buried!' Bob collared the excited man, exchanged a few words with him, and then called out to me—'Send out Hamilton, Pestle, and the stretcher at once, and you know what besides.' Away he sped over the hill towards Campbell's. This was a claim consisting of eight men's ground, originally taken up by Campbell and party as alluvial. They had not sunk far when they met the cap of a gold-bearing reef. When the fall occurred the party were driving for this reef at the level opening out from the shaft, at a depth of 300 feet. Water was oozing from the 'face,' usually an indication that the body of stone is not far distant, and in eagerness to verify the sign, and knowing little about 'reefing,' they had neglected to properly timber up the drive. This was the cause of the trouble. The timber supports had given way, and three out of the four men on day shift—the fourth was on top at the windlass—were entombed. Bob was not the first on the ground, but he was the first to go down to reconnoitre—the others seemed to have lost their wits. Just as I arrived at the mouth of the shaft with the doctor, who, for a wonder was sober, Bob was hauled up. By this time hundreds were on the ground, and every eye was on Bob as he swung himself clear of the shaft. You see, they knew what he couldn't do it would be useless to attempt. Bob put a question or two to the mates of the buried men, so as to learn the bearings, and then looking round, he named four others to go down with him—the biggest and strongest on the field. There was risk, of course, but those chaps never gave it a thought. As he called them, they stepped out proudly.

"'We'll have them out in a couple of hours,' he said, 'and alive, if they haven't been killed by the fall. They'll have enough air for that time.' And then, as he was putting his foot in the noose, he turned and said to me, 'Old Pestle, mind you have everything right up here for them.' These were the last words ever heard from him in his unbroken manhood. There was the modest masterfulness in his tone, and there was the thoughtfulness for others in his words. Always true to himself, was Bob.

"What happened next I can't clearly tell. We on top sent a man down to the bottom of the shaft at intervals to learn how things were going on, and he always returned with the news that they were working famously. Two of the five were kept timbering, and the others relieved each other every ten minutes with the pick at the face. Bob took double turn though, besides giving an eye to the timbering. It was near the middle of the second hour, when the signal to haul up was hurriedly given, and a cry came up that we made out to be that they had got the men. First one, then two, then three, bleeding, maimed, and unconscious miners were brought to the surface. They had all been saved alive, and Hamilton gave hopes of their recovery. We were so intent on the rescued that we forgot the rescuers for a time. Only two of the five had come up; they told us that Bob and the others had stopped to make the timber 'sets' as tight as possible. All at once there roared up the shaft what might have been the explosion of a ship's broadside. Every face of the two thousand then on the ground blanched at the sound, for we all knew that the waters had broken in. Quick and sharp came the signal to pull. The men were at the bottom of the shaft. A dozen arms went to the windlass; round it flew as quickly as it could be made to do, although it was evident there was a double load. Fifty heads bent down into the darkness of the pit, and strained to catch a glimpse of the men. At last they could be made out. Bob was left behind. 'What's the matter? Where's Half-Crown?' was the cry. 'The water's in. Waitin' down below; he made us come first.' There was a grim silence then, and an unspoken thought in all minds that these men had no right to come before Bob. I had it myself, though, of course, it was unjust. The fellows were barely level with the mouth when they were pulled off the rope to which they were hanging, one above the other, and then before any one could speak there was a man, who was known only as 'Yank,' rattling down the shaft. The men just come up wanted to tell how it all happened, but nobody listened. Every soul there, I believe, was praying that 'Yank' might get down before it was too late. Yank, I should tell you, was a fellow who, when he first reached

the Creek, swore he wouldn't know Bob. He had to, the
boys made him, and broke his leg in doing it; but so far
from feeling sore against Bob, he loved him like a dog.
We waited and waited, and not a sign came. Of course,
we could not see whether the water had risen in the shaft,
for all we knew Yank might himself be drowning. We had
lowered him till he had jerked the rope once—that was
to stop—and it was certain, as all the rope had not paid
out, that he had not reached the mouth of the drive. We
could hear nothing except the noise of the water,
sometimes soughing, sometimes booming. At last, it was
exactly six o'clock, I recollect hearing somebody say,
came the two sharp jerks. When the strain was felt on the
rope the word was passed round that the burden was
double. That meant that Yank had got Bob. It seemed
ages before we landed them, for Yank had often to stop
the haulage. When we did—great God!—Yank was seen
to be dripping wet and covered with blood, holding Bob
in his arms. We thought Half-Crown was dead. His back
must have been broken as he grasped the side of the shaft
in endeavouring to escape the inrush of water. A log, so
Yank said, of one of the timber sets, must have been
propelled by the terrible force of the stream against the
body of the poor lad. We undid the cords that bound Bob
to the rope and to Yank as tenderly as we could—It was
a marvellous thing how Yank had managed to fasten
them in the midst of the horror and the darkness—and

then we laid him on a stretcher. The people drew back to give him air, and to let the doctor examine him. When Hamilton looked up, we read death in his glance, and groans and sobs, that could not be stifled, arose from the crowd. The sound disturbed Bob. He opened his eyes and feebly glanced round. I went to his side, and asked him did he know me. His lips parted as if to speak, and I knelt down to listen. For some minutes he could not utter a word, but with an effort he lifted his hand and stroked my face. I have had rather a rough-and-tumble existence. Mr. Strathing, and some curious experiences, but nothing in my life went to my heart like that feeble stroking. I was that touched, that but for fear of distressing him I could have burst out crying. At last he found his voice, and the doctor said it was a miracle he ever spoke again. As it was, his words were sighed forth, and nobody heard them but me. 'Pestle,' he said, 'old friend Pestle,' and here he had to make a long pause, and in a sense I was glad of it; to think that with his dying breath he should refer to our friendship! 'Papers in tent—write—home ones—fondest love all—all, Pestle, mind, all!'

"The 'all,' sir, was uttered distinctly, as if he meant to convey that some one was included whom others might have thought undeserving of remembrance. You will know, doubtless, whether it was so or not. The effort to emphasize it, and to make me understand, hurried the fatal moment. We thought, indeed, that he had already gone. But, in a while, he revived. Again I put my ear to his lips, afraid a syllable of his precious speech would be lost. 'Bury—Grampians,' was all I could make out of the whisper, however, and he turned his head as though he would look on those blue hills once more. There they lay in the west, steeped in the splendour of a glorious sunset; but he could not see them, because the silent throng stood between him and them. I waved my hand. The crowd, as if by instinct, understood, and, with scarcely a sound, moved right and left. He saw the hills then, but I don't think he saw the people. Again we thought he had left us. But no; his lips moved, and I caught, 'I'm going west too, old Pestle; going west too.' Another long pause, broken only by the sough of the wind, the creaking of a chain dangling from a poppet-head close by, and the sobs under breath from the crowd. Then he seemed to recall the present, and murmured, 'Remember—all—boys, Pestle. Give Half-Crown's love!' The words came with great gasps. Another interval, and then, 'Who saved me?' he asked. Saved! with his life ebbing like that. Oh, it was pitiful. I whispered in reply, 'Yank!' and pulled Yank to the stretcher side. Something of your dear lad's brightness came back, as, smiling faintly, he said, 'Ah, Yank! sorry—been "interdooced"?' Yank broke out crying like a child. The brightness soon faded. For some time he lay still with his eyes open, peering into the heavens, with a far-away look. Suddenly he rose, as if he saw some one in the distance, and in a sharp tone of pleasure—yes, it was pleasure, there was no tinge of pain in it—exclaimed, 'Mother! Lois!' The last name he repeated more softly, though scarcely more tenderly, and then he fell back into my arms—dead; I closed his eyes.

"There, I have written it all down. Till I commenced to write I did not think I remembered more than a solitary detail or two—I have been dazed since it happened. But, I seemed to have noticed nearly everything in spite of myself. And perhaps it is best that you should have all the particulars of the noble fellow's last hours.

"We buried him today in a narrow valley of the Grampians; and Petre, one of the English Petres, a complete scamp, but one of the warmest admirers of Bob, recollected a talk he had once had with Bob when hunting in the hills. Bob had pointed out a beautiful spot in a small valley at the foot of a cascade, and remarked that 'he would like to be buried there.' 'What! not in England?' Petre had exclaimed. Bob had said— 'If I may not be buried there with honour, I would sooner rest here;' but in such a tone that Petre dropped the subject. He told me of the conversation the night Bob died, and we agreed that he should see if he could find the place. He went off the same night, camped out, and having found the spot returned next day for men to dig the poor boy's grave. He came in again last evening to act as our guide today.

"This morning at daybreak, every man on the field who could walk, or ride, or get carried, seventeen miles, followed Bob to his grave in the midst of the hills. Many women went, too; among them Mrs. Hamilton. As the coffin was being lowered, she placed on it a wreath of golden wattle and pure white roses intermingled, saying, 'From his mother.' It was a kindly token that spoke the thoughts of most there, and if fitly symbolized, so it seemed to me, what the dear lad was. The sweet perfume of our homely English flower mingled with the rich odour of the brilliant Australian blossom, just as Bob's life had a fragrance that was neither English altogether, nor Australian altogether, but both combined.

"Thousands were in the procession. Few of England's greatest have had an equally, none a more honourable funeral. Many of those who walked out could not, of course, return today. They keep watch by Bob in this his first night in the silent valley.

"A piece of the holly was placed in his coffin.

"The miners have already subscribed to erect a monument over him, but we will do nothing till we hear from you.

"Because I write this, and because Bob asked me in his latest words to see to his papers, you will understand that I was more intimate with him than any other person here. I knew his name; no one else did. The whole field called him 'Half-Crown.' This was because of a story that he had promised some one in the old land to live upon half-a-crown a week until he achieved a certain object. If it was possible for any man to do such a thing, Bob was the man.

"Needless to say, I have not examined his papers and effects more closely than necessary to discover your address and to settle his affairs here. All his belongings go to you by the mail steamer that carries this. The shipping papers will be transmitted to you in due course by my Melbourne agents.

"Pray command me in all things that you desire to be done.

"Petre has just brought me in a hastily-drawn sketch of the spot where we have laid your son. I enclose it.

"I have nothing more to say, except this—if you will pardon me for saying it—that, poorer as the world may be without Bob, it is immeasurably the richer for his having lived.

"Very sincerely yours.

"SAMUEL PESTLE."

EPILOGUE

IN THE HEART of the Grampians, where two hills meet, and form a narrow triangular vale, is Robert Strathing's grave. Across the freestone obelisk at its head flit the shadows of giant gums, in whose leaves are gathered the wind-whispered monodies of centuries. By its foot pass tiny rivulets from the pool where drops, with a foamy plash, the silvery stream of a waterfall. The cadence of the dropping water and the rustling of the trees unite in a musical murmur that sounds to a listener like a never-ending sequence of sighs. On the face of the obelisk is inlaid a marble slab, on which may be read the following inscription—ROBERT STRATHING,

Aged 25 years. Here he takes his rest—The drear music of an unjust blame Moves him no more. Heaven itself Breathes low his lullaby.

Over the epitaph is sculptured with rare skill a representation of the obverse and reverse of a coin encircled by a wreath, in which wattle-blossom and roses have been linked by the delicate touch of the artist. Lois herself brought out the tablet, which was graven and carved for her by one whose genius was before long to receive the well-earned tributes of fame and wealth, to whom Bob had endeared himself in college days.

Once every year, just after the spring has sent forth her couriers of sound and colour to tell of the glories and the sweetness of resurrected nature, and when "the tides of grass" in the valley "are breaking into foam of flowers," a lady comes from the quiet Tasmanian village where she lives, and makes a pilgrimage to the grave. Old Pestle, whose right to the adjective now none will question, drives her out to the sequestered spot. Together they stand by the grave-side for a brief space. Then Pestle leaves her alone; it may be for an hour. As she hears his slow step returning to warn her that if they would escape the darkness, they must depart, she turns and kisses the stone and sod, pulls a few flowers from the pied mound, which she folds tenderly within a little case she has brought with her for the purpose, and tells him she is ready. The poor of Stawell district wish Half-Crown Bob's sweetheart would come oftener, for old Pestle, after each recurring visit, adds another function to his many offices by acting as almoner for Lois' benefactions. Lois is alone now. First, the old man passed away, and then his wife. Bob's death preceded theirs by a few months only, for Pestle's letter gave them their death-blow. Lois, now chief partner in Carlyon and Strathing, waits to follow them. She could have married along since; but she will never give to another the homage and the tenderness won by her dead hero, to whom, at last, she does justice. And she lives now but for the poor and suffering.

FINIS